megabat

Daniel can't wait for his birthday party: games, cake, friends and presents!

Megabat also can't wait for Daniel's birthday: games, smooshfruit, friends and presents!

Daniel explains that only the person celebrating the birthday gets presents.

Megabat is less enthused—that is none fair!

Daniel hides Megabat in his hat so no one will see him.

Megabat doesn't care for this. Now he won't win any games!

Daniel gets frustrated with Megabat and leaves him inside.

Megabat has a small tantrum . . . with a BIG result.

What will Daniel do when he sees what Megabat did? Does Megabat even deserve Daniel as a friend? And what secret are Talia, Birdgirl and Daniel keeping from him? Birthdays aren't nearly as fun as Megabat thought they'd be.

Tundra Books, an imprint of Penguin Random House Canada Young Readers,
a division of Penguin Random House of Canada Limited

Library and Archives Canada Cataloguing in Publication

Title: Megabat and the not-happy birthday / Anna Humphrey ; [illustrations by] Kass Reich
Other titles: Not-happy birthday

MAY - '21   Names: Humphrey, Anna, author. | Reich, Kass, illustrator.
Series: Humphrey, Anna. Megabat (Series)
Description: Series statement: Megabat

Identifiers: Canadiana (print) 20200182188 | Canadiana (ebook) 20200182196
ISBN 9780735266049 (hardcover) | ISBN 9780735266056 (EPUB)

Classification: LCC PS8615.U457 M44 2021 | DDC jC813/.6—dc23

Published simultaneously in the United States of America by Tundra Books of
Northern New York, an imprint of Penguin Random House Canada Young Readers,
a division of Penguin Random House of Canada Limited

Library of Congress Control Number: 2020931804

Edited by Samantha Swenson
Designed by John Martz
The artwork in this book was rendered in graphite.
The text was set in Caslon 540 LT Std.

Printed and bound in the United States of America

www.penguinrandomhouse.ca

1   2   3   4   5   25   24   23   22   21

Penguin
Random House
tundra   TUNDRA BOOKS

ANNA HUMPHREY
illustrated by KASS REICH

MEGA
BAT

AND THE
NOT-HAPPY BIRTHDAY

tundra

For Devan, Arik, Sophie
and Rowan

THE FACE WINDOWS

Daniel got the wonderful face windows the day after he and Megabat got lost on the sugar-bush field trip.

He was *not* happy about them.

"I'm not wearing these dumb-looking things! Mom and Dad can't make me!"

The face windows, which Daniel had just tossed angrily onto his bed, were round with reddish edges. Megabat tapped a tiny talon against one of the clear parts. It was hard and shiny, like the pane of glass in the backyard shed he shared with his beloved—a pigeon named Birdgirl. Only, when he peered through the glass, instead of looking regular, the world tilted and stretched in a way that made him delightfully dizzy.

Megabat wrapped his wings around the face windows and hobbled across the bed to offer them to his friend. "Looking, Daniel!" He peered through one lens again, wobbled, and then fell down. "It's being ker-bobbling! Like when we's swirl on the swings."

Daniel crossed his arms and turned away. "Glasses might be fun for you,

Megabat, but they're not fun for me.
And none of this would have happened
if you hadn't made us late for the bus.
I'm still mad at you. So just leave me
alone, okay? Go work on your coloring
or something."

Megabat hopped off the bed and
stomped to the corner. It had been a

whole day since he'd made the clock mistake. Wasn't Daniel *ever* going to forgive him?

The problem had started on the hayride.

"When I drop you off in the maple forest, see if you can spot our blue jays," the tractor driver had said, as the wagon bump-bumped along. She pointed off to one side and Megabat, who was hiding in the folded-over part of Daniel's winter hat, caught sight of a little wooden bird, hidden in the branches of a tree.

"There are fifteen. If you find them all, come see me and I'll give you a prize."

At that, Megabat's large ears had perked up. He'd always wanted a prize!

Daniel's friend and next-door neighbor Talia had one. She'd won it for doing the very best tricks and flips at a gymnastics competition. It was tall and golden with a little person on top.

"Oooooh! Prizes are being spunktacular," Megabat said.

Talia, who was sitting in the wagon beside Daniel, looked up and held one finger to her lips, reminding Megabat to be quiet. Bats weren't allowed on field trips—or at school—and if Mrs. Gallagher or any of the other kids discovered Megabat, there'd be a huge fuss.

Finally, the wagon came to a stop.

"Everyone, meet back at the bus in half an hour," Mrs. Gallagher instructed. "That's one-thirty exactly." She pointed out a big clock on the outside wall of the sugar shack.

The kids wandered off in different directions. First, Daniel and Megabat lined up in front of a lady in a bonnet who was handing out little cups of syrup. It tasted like the sweetest fruit nectar.

"Mmmmmmm. Sweerup," Megabat said as he slurped the last drop.

Just then, Talia walked over. "We're going to check out the gift shop." She was with her friends Nico and Ella. "Wanna come?"

"Sure," Daniel answered, but when Nico and Ella turned their backs, Megabat hung down from the side of Daniel's hat and stuck his snout into his friend's ear.

"Daniel! Let's doing the birds hunt!"

Daniel startled at the tickly feeling. Then he reached up and poked Megabat back underneath his hat.

Megabat popped out again. "Peeeeeeeeeeeze! There's being a splendiferous prize!"

Daniel couldn't help smiling at Megabat's excitement. "Okay," he said softly.

"Actually," he said, loudly enough for Talia's friends to hear, "I didn't bring money, so I'm going to do that bird hunt thing." He winked at Talia and pointed at his hat. She understood.

"Right. That sounds fun too," she said. "See you at the bus."

Because Megabat lived with a pigeon, he knew he'd have a special talent for spotting birds—even wooden ones. The first eleven were easy to find in trees and on rooftops. Daniel noticed three more nailed to benches, but that still left one last bird: a tricky one.

"What time is it?" Daniel squinted at the big round clock as they passed the sugar shack.

Megabat studied the clock. He was just learning to tell time.

"Hmmmmm. The baby stick is being nearish the one," he reported.

"Okay," Daniel said. "What about the minute hand? The big one."

"The biggish stick is being . . ." Megabat remembered that one-thirty was bus time—but there wasn't a number thirty on the clock. The big stick was almost at six . . . and six was a much smaller number than thirty. They had plenty of time left to find the tricky bird!

"The biggish stick is saying six minutes," he answered with authority.

So they kept searching . . . and when Megabat saw a sign up ahead that read DO NOT ENTER, he thought of Birdgirl. The pigeon always wanted to go where she wasn't allowed—whether that was inside Daniel's bedroom to play checkers or near the fancy new bird feeder Daniel's mother filled for the sparrows. If the last wooden bird was anything like Birdgirl, it was certainly somewhere behind that sign.

"Thattaway!" Megabat pointed with one wingtip.

Daniel and Megabat never did find the tricky bird, but they discovered a swamp that soaked Daniel's snow boots, some railroad tracks and a bunch of fallen logs—one of which they were sitting on when Mrs. Gallagher and the tractor driver finally found them.

After that, there was some scolding

from the teacher and some explaining
about not being able to see the clock or
the signs from Daniel. The tractor driver
felt sorry when Daniel cried, so she gave
him the bird hunt prize anyway.

That was when Megabat felt like
crying.

"Ubsolutely un-splendiferous." He
shook his little head now as he sat now in

the corner of Daniel's room, scribbling angrily on the prize, which was *not* a solid gold trophy but a photocopied coloring book filled with pictures about the sugar bush.

"You can say that again," Daniel said miserably. "I hate these ugly glasses!"

2

YOU ARE UNVITED

Even though Daniel thought his face
windows were ugly, no one else did. In
fact, when he wore them to school the
next day, lots of people said nice things.

"Looking very distinguished," Mrs.
Barton, the gym teacher, remarked as
she walked by with an armload of
badminton rackets.

"Aren't those nice, Daniel!" Mrs.

Gallagher commented later that day as she passed back that morning's math quizzes. "And look! Now that you can see the questions on the board, you got ten out of ten!"

She'd put a scratch-and-sniff sticker at the top of the page. It had a picture of a piece of toast with purple jelly and the words *Grape Job!* Megabat longed to lick it.

"I wish I had glasses!" Nico said on the playground at recess. "They make you look smart. Like a scientist."

Megabat, who was nestled inside Daniel's coat pocket, frowned. He wished he had face windows of his own. People would call him a very beautiful,

brainy bat indeed. Perhaps he'd even get
a sticker!

　　He didn't have long to think about it,
though, because he remembered
something exciting.

"Daniel!" Megabat poked his friend's tummy through his coat to get his attention.

"What?" Daniel whispered into his pocket.

"The unvitations!"

"Oh, right. Thanks, Megabat!" Daniel took a card out of his other pocket and turned around. "Hey, Nico. My birthday party is next week. Can you come?"

Megabat pressed his ear to the fabric of Daniel's coat, waiting for Nico's answer.

"You're invited to Daniel Misumi's All-You-Can-Eat Sugar Cereal Pig-Out Party," Nico read. "Saturday at four o'clock. Cool! I'll be there."

Megabat wriggled with excitement.
He loved parties more than watermelon
(which he called buttermelon) . . . more
than going to the car wash . . . more than
twirly slides . . . more than anything! And
he'd never been to a real birthday party
before! The year before, Daniel hadn't had
one. Instead, they went on a trip to the
zoo with Daniel's parents, since he'd just
moved and hadn't met many friends yet.

"What do you want for a present?"
Nico asked.

Megabat gasped. *Presents!?* Daniel
hadn't told him there would be presents!

"I don't know," Daniel answered.
"Maybe some new art markers? Or
whatever, really."

Megabat poked furiously at Daniel's tummy.

"See you in a bit," Daniel said to Nico. "I need to . . . uh . . . find Ella. What is it?" he whispered to Megabat after he'd walked a safe distance away.

"Mine wants a hummonica." Then, remembering his manners, Megabat added, "Peeze!"

"What?" Daniel asked.

"A hummonica. Like the man on the sidewalk who hads the hat!"

They'd seen the man in the summer, playing his small silver instrument on a street corner near the doughnut shop. When he hummed into it, it made beautiful buzzy noises and—best of

all—people passing by had clapped their hands and put shiny money into his hat. If Megabat had a hummonica, he would play it day and night. Everyone would cheer.

"A harmonica?" Daniel asked.

Megabat nodded. "For mine present!"

"You don't get a present," Daniel said.

Megabat blinked up at him.

"It's not your birthday," Daniel explained. "At a birthday party, only the birthday person gets presents."

"None fair!" Megabat proclaimed. It was the most outrageous thing he'd ever heard!

"Shhhh," Daniel said as a teacher walked past. "Birthday means the day you were born." Daniel went on. "It's fair because everyone gets a turn to be the birthday person, but this time it's my turn."

"When will it be being Megabat's turn?" the bat asked.

"I don't know." Daniel shrugged. "When were you born?"

Megabat scritched one ear and thought hard but, try as he might, he couldn't remember being born.

"Hey, Ella!" Daniel called across the playground. "Wanna come to my birthday party on Saturday?"

And off they went to deliver another invitation to Daniel's party where only Daniel would get presents. Megabat grumbled to himself inside the coat pocket. "Most none fair."

THE PIÑATA AND
THE SQUIRREL

All week Daniel and Megabat prepared
for Daniel's all-you-can-eat breakfast
cereal birthday party. Even Megabat had
to admit, that part was fun.

Daniel's mom took them to the
grocery store and—from inside Daniel's
pocket—Megabat helped choose the
boxes of crunchy, brightly colored cereal

the guests would eat. His favorite was the one with rainbow loops. They also picked balloons and streamers and ordered a cake with icing the color of a clear blue sky.

On Thursday after school, they made the piñata. It was a kind of candy-holding sculpture that would look just like the big-nosed bird on the box of rainbow loops cereal. Talia came over to help, and because the work was messy and the weather was warm, they worked outside.

"I think that's almost enough," Talia told Birdgirl, who was helping too.

"Coo-woo." The pigeon emerged from the pile of newspaper she was shredding and ruffled her feathers.

Meanwhile, Megabat was stirring the paste—a special mixture made of flour and water. "Most gloopy," he said, enjoying the squish of it.

"I'll get some boxes from the recycling bin to make the beak!" Daniel said. "Hey, Talia. Can you help me?"

"Mine can help!" Megabat offered. He loved helping.

"Thanks, Megabat," Daniel said. "But it would be better if Talia came. She's . . . um . . . good at carrying stuff. Because she's got such strong arms from gymnastics."

"Are these boxes really that heavy?" Talia asked.

"Just come with me," Daniel urged. Talia shrugged and followed Daniel to the shed where the recycling was kept.

"Humph," Megabat said—and, being his beloved, Birdgirl understood. She nuzzled her face into one of his leathery wings to let him know she thought he'd be very good at carrying boxes too. That made Megabat feel better.

"Perhaps we should starting?" he asked Birdgirl.

Daniel had already explained how to make the piñata. First, they'd dip the newspaper pieces into the paste. Then, they would smooth each piece onto the cardboard shape they'd made for the toucan's body. Easy!

Birdgirl, who was extremely crafty, did the first dip—but it didn't go as planned.

"Coo-woo!" she cried, sputtering a beakful of paste. She shook her whole body, trying to free the strip of newspaper that had glued itself to the side of her head.

"Mine will helping yours." Megabat plucked the newspaper off, but it got stuck to his wingtip. He flapped. Finally, it came loose, landing with a splat on the picnic table.

"Trying other ones," he suggested.

The bat and the pigeon dipped new bits of paper, but Megabat's got attached to his foot, and Birdgirl's ended up on her forehead.

That was when they heard the chittering laughter coming from the top of the fence.

Chichichichi.

It was one of the pesky puffer rats

who lived in the yard. Daniel called them *kwirls*. This one was gray and brown with a fat white tummy.

"Oh, being quiet, Kwirl!" Megabat said.

He grabbed the gluey newspaper off his foot, only to have it stick to his wing. This time, when he shook it loose, it flew across the table and landed on Birdgirl's head, covering her eyes. The pigeon bobbed frantically, and the squirrel laughed even harder.

"Hey! Is not so easy-peasy!" Megabat hollered.

The squirrel skittered down the fence to investigate. He inched his way across the picnic table, twitching his tail, and sniffed at the bowl of paste.

"If yours thinks yours can making a better pine-yatta," Megabat invited, "going rights ahead."

Kwirl puffed his chest at the challenge. He picked up a piece of shredded newspaper, dipped it into the paste and applied it easily to the cardboard shape, smoothing it down with his grabby little paws. Then he wriggled his nose smugly, picked up another piece of paper and hopped onto the side of the bowl to dip it.

Megabat shouldn't have been surprised. Puffer rats were always showing off . . . whether they were swinging upside down from trees or leaping fearlessly from rooftop to rooftop.

Only, sometimes—*THUNK!*—they went a little too far and too fast.

Kwirl's weight tipped the bowl of paste, and the flour-and-water mixture spilled onto the picnic table, washing him over the side in a slippery river of gloop.

"Kwirl!" Megabat rushed to the edge of the table. "Is yours oka-hay?"

But when he peered down, the squirrel was lying on his back in the brownish grass, chittering with uncontrollable laughter. And before Megabat or Birdgirl could blink, he'd leapt back onto the table and was sliding through the paste to do it again.

Megabat looked at Birdgirl.

Birdgirl looked at Megabat.

It *did* look fun—which was why, when Daniel and Talia came back from the shed a minute later carrying the extra cardboard, they found not only the squirrel, but also the bat and the pigeon completely covered in paste.

"Megabat!?" Daniel gasped. "Birdgirl! What are you doing?"

"Gloop glidiiiiiing!" Megabat called out as he slid past on his back. "Yours should trying it, Daniel! Is—oof!" He reached the edge of the table and plunged off into the grass. "Most slipperish!"

Daniel's face loomed above him. "Megabat," he scolded, but he was laughing. "You guys made a huge mess."

Megabat flew back up to the table. His wings were covered in a fine fur of brown grass blades, and the gloopy paste was starting to stiffen in places.

"You're going to have to clean this up," Talia said, dipping one finger into the guck.

"But, it wasn't being ours's idea. It was the—" Megabat looked left and right, about to blame Kwirl, but the puffer rat was already dashing away down the fence.

"You're both going to need a shower too," Daniel went on.

"I'll go get the garden hose," Talia offered.

"Wait, Talia!" he said. "I just had

another idea." He whispered something in her ear.

Talia smiled.

"Whats?" Megabat asked. "Mine wants to knowing the whisper!"

"Sorry, Megabat," Daniel said. "It's a secret."

Megabat grimaced, causing the dried paste on his face to crack a little. He didn't like whispers—at least, not when they weren't for his ears.

And, a minute later, he liked the cold shower he and Birdgirl had to take in hose water even less.

THE PARTY

The next day, Daniel and Talia traded more secrets at school—and on Saturday afternoon, when Talia came early to help decorate, Megabat felt even more left out.

The friends were in the dining room, blowing up balloons, when Megabat flapped onto the table.

"Ah-HEM!" He struck a pose with one wingtip behind his head.

"Hi, Megabat," Talia said between puffs as she blew into a green balloon. It was already so big and round that Megabat could hardly see her face behind it. Perhaps she couldn't see him either.

"Yes, it's being mine!" Megabat announced. "A most dustinguished bat."

"Just a sec, Megabat. I have to tie this. It's the hardest part." When Talia had finished knotting the balloon, she looked up at Megabat and laughed—hardly the reaction he'd been hoping for.

"Look, Daniel," she said. "You aren't the only one with glasses anymore."

Daniel lowered the blue balloon he'd been blowing up and smiled at Megabat.

"Hey, those look pretty sharp!" he said.

Megabat wrinkled his snout. "Theys isn't being sharp! Theys is being bendy!"

Birdgirl had helped Megabat make the bat-sized glasses using two twist ties. "Theys making mine smart, like a scientist."

To demonstrate, Megabat walked around the green balloon Talia had set down on the table. "Hmmmmm." He examined it from all angles. "Mine will now be making some scientific *lobstervations.*" He used the big important word Mrs. Gallagher said when they did experiments in class.

Daniel and Talia seemed impressed, so Megabat went on. "Greenish balloons is mine favorites because theys looks muchly like buttermelons."

He sniffed the balloon. "But theys is not smelling like buttermelons. Does theys tasting like buttermelons? Lets us testing the *high-poppa-niss.*"

"Megabat, no!" Daniel yelled, just as
the bat bit into the balloon.

BANG!

Megabat jumped so high that his
twist-tie glasses fell off. And Priscilla the

cat, who'd been curled up in a sunny spot on the couch, glared at him for disturbing her rest before flouncing away to hide.

Talia laughed at Megabat's shocked expression. "Don't worry. I've got strong lungs. I'll just blow up another one."

"Wait though," Daniel said, as Talia reached into the bag. "Not green. We should save those." He gave Talia a wink.

Megabat picked up the floppy pieces of the broken one. "But mine wants a greenish balloon."

"Sorry, Megabat. We need those for, um . . ." Daniel paused. "An art project Birdgirl wants to do."

"Peeze! Just one!" he pleaded.

46

"I already said no, Megabat," Daniel answered firmly. Megabat stomped his tiny foot, but Daniel didn't pay any attention.

The doorbell rang.

"I bet that's Nico and Ella. Stay under here so nobody sees you, okay?" Daniel put Megabat on his head, then plopped a cone-shaped party hat on top.

"Happy birthday, Daniel!"

Megabat could see out a crack where the two sides of the cardboard hat joined. Not only were Nico and Ella standing in the doorway, but so were Sophie from across the street and Arik from Daniel's Ranger Scouts group. Arik and Sophie were carrying brightly colored gift bags with crinkly paper coming out the top—and Nico and Ella were each holding one end of a big box covered in stars.

Daniel showed them where to put the presents. Then it was time for games. First up was the great necklace race.

Daniel explained: "Everyone gets a long piece of yarn, and we see how many Fruity Loops we can put on in five minutes. The person with the longest necklace wins."

Arik had fast fingers. When he was done, his necklace looped four times around his neck.

Next, they played Alphabet-Cereal Boggle.

"Everyone gets a bowl of alphabet-shaped cereal," Talia instructed. "We've got five minutes to spell the most words possible."

At first, Megabat liked that one. He peeked out from under the party hat and helped his friend when everyone was busy looking at their letters.

"*Bat!*" Megabat whispered. Daniel spotted the letters and arranged them.

"Thanks," he whispered. He pushed Megabat back in.

Megabat popped back out. "*Burp!*"

"Nice! But shhhh."

Megabat popped out a third time. "Oh! *Tede!*"

Nico looked up from the cereal he'd

been arranging, and Megabat only just
managed to duck back under the hat in
time. "What did you say, Daniel?"

"Sorry . . ." Daniel answered. "Just talking to myself. It helps me find words."

Daniel touched the *T* with his finger then rearranged some of the other letters, but he couldn't seem to find it.

Finally, Megabat had to spell into his ear. "*T-E-D-E*. Like yours's favorite tede bear!"

"Shh! That's not how you spell *teddy*," Daniel whispered.

Sophie spelled eleven words, including long ones like *international* and beautiful ones like *allergy*. She won that game.

Finally, they went outside for Crazy Corn-Pop Toss. One partner stood behind a line while the other tried to throw bits of cereal into their partner's mouth. Birdgirl came out from the shed to eat dropped pieces, and even Kwirl had a good snack, but Megabat had to stay hidden under Daniel's hat where it was no fun at all.

Talia, Daniel, Nico and Ella tied. Then it was time for prizes. Everyone got a shiny gold medal on a rope. Everyone except Megabat.

He couldn't imagine the party could get any worse, but it did.

"Let's open presents."

The kids raced to the living room. Talia gave Daniel a Star Wars board game.

Arik got Daniel a plant with teeth. "It's a Venus flytrap," he explained.

Sophie's gift was a make-your-own balloon animals kit.

He liked them all, but you could tell the last one was his favorite. "You've *got* to be kidding me!" Daniel said, when he unwrapped the big box from Nico and Ella. "A Boogie Bot!"

"It comes with twenty-five pre-loaded dances. Plus, it's the LOL version, so it knows more than fifty jokes," Ella said proudly.

Just as Daniel had promised, there were no presents for Megabat, or for anyone else, but the other kids didn't seem to mind. They brought the robot up to Daniel's room, worked together to build it, then crowded around as Daniel

fit two big batteries into its back and flipped the switch.

The robot blinked its big, round eyes open and looked left and right.

"Greetings!" It bent its knees stiffly and wiggled from side to side. "I'm Boogie Bot, your personal programmable disco dude. Choose an option. Are you ready to boogie or would you like to hear a joke?"

"Joke!" Arik shouted.

"What's a robot's favorite type of music?" Boogie Bot blinked twice. "Heavy metal!" Loud, clangy sounds came from somewhere in its belly and it started to nod angrily. The kids laughed, but underneath the party hat, Megabat frowned and covered his ears to block out the not-nice noise.

"That's funny!" the robot said, then it laughed at its own joke.

"Tell another joke!" Sophie said.

"Okay," Boogie Bot answered. "Why did the robot get annoyed?"

"I don't know. Why?" Daniel asked.

Boogie Bot blinked. The buttons on its arms lit up. "Because someone kept pushing its buttons."

The kids laughed again.

The robot laughed too. "That's funny," it said.

But it wasn't. Megabat knew a *much* better joke. He scritched Daniel's head to get his attention. Daniel walked into the corner, took off his hat and flipped it upside down so Megabat got scooped inside. "What is it now?!" he whispered, a little impatiently.

"Telling the joke about the fly bug!" Megabat urged.

"Maybe later, okay? First we want to see the robot dance."

"Mine can dance!"

"I know, Megabat."

"Mine can dance goodly!"

"Yes, you're a great dancer," Daniel whispered, but it didn't sound like he really meant it.

Megabat gave a sad little sniff, and Daniel must have felt bad for him.

"Okay . . . If I tell the joke about

the fly, will you let me go play with the robot?"

Megabat nodded, so Daniel flipped the hat back onto his head.

"Hey, guys! I know a good one."

Megabat wriggled in anticipation. This was the best joke in the world. "What do you call a fly with no wings?"

"I don't know," Ella said. "What?"

"A walk," Daniel answered.

Underneath the hat, Megabat laughed so hard that holding it in made tears stream down his face. But when he peered out the hat crack to see the kids' reactions, only Nico was smiling. "Ha!" he said. "My grandpa told me that joke last week."

The other kids were gathered around the robot watching it do a dance called the tango.

Just then, Daniel's mother called up the stairs.

"If you guys want to break the piñata, now would be the time. Then we'll have the cereal pig-out and eat cake."

"Okay!" Daniel called back. "Come on, guys. Let's go outside."

Megabat tugged hard on his friend's hair.

"I'll be there in a second." Daniel let everyone else go ahead.

"Ouch! Megabat! What *now*?"

"Mine knows a laughinger joke!

Telling it to yours's friends," he said. "What's being brown and sticky?"

"I don't know, Megabat." Daniel sighed. "What?"

"A stick!" Megabat said. "Getting it?"

Daniel groaned. "I get it, but it's not funny."

That hurt Megabat's feelings. "It's is *so* funny. Yours is being mean!" He stomped his tiny foot against Daniel's palm.

"Okay, that's it." Daniel said firmly. "I've had just about enough of you for today. First, the big fuss over the green balloon, then sulking because you didn't get a medal, and now this. It's MY party,

and I want to go spend time with my guests, okay?"

"Harumph." Mcgabat crossed his wings over his chest and stuck out his batty bottom lip.

"Harumph yourself," Daniel answered. "If you're going to keep pouting, you can just stay here—and stay out of trouble."

So Megabat *did* stay there . . . but staying out of trouble was the much harder part.

BOOGIE BOT

After Daniel left, Megabat stomped around the bedroom saying angry things in his loudest voice.

"This is being the ungoodliest party EVER."

He marched under the bed, kicked at a dust cloud and came out the other side.

"None greenish balloons." He listed off the problems on his wingtips. "None prizes and none presents for Megabat. None fun at all!" He whirled around and accidentally bumped into the Boogie Bot, which was sitting in the middle of the room where it had no business being.

"Robot!" he said sternly. "Yours's jokes are being unfunny. Nobody likings yours, oka-hay? Going away!" The robot blinked. *"Just go!"* Megabat yelled in frustration.

"Did someone say *disco*?" the robot answered.

Music started to play from its tummy. "I love to boogie woogie disco-style." The robot's arms moved stiffly, back and forth, up and down.

Megabat watched it, frowning.

"I'm a great dancer!" the robot said, when it was done. "Do you like to dance too?"

"For fact," Megabat said, "mine is a splendiferous dancer!" Even though the robot had somehow managed to out-joke him, there was no way it could out-dance him. "Watching this!"

Megabat swept his wings back and forth dramatically and twirled on the spot. "Taking that," he proclaimed when he was done. Then, feeling angrier than ever, he called it a bad name "Doo-doo robot!"

Boogie Bot blinked, misunderstanding. "Did someone say *do the robot?*" It laughed tauntingly. "When it comes to *that* dance, people say I'm a natural!"

The robot rolled back and forth holding its arms like the letter *L* and flipping them up and down in time to the music. It finished with a smug smile. "I'm a great dancer," it bragged again.

"Robot." Megabat shook his head. "Mines sorry, but yours's dancing is being a joke!"

"A joke?" the robot answered. "Sure!" Its lights flashed. "How do bees brush their hair?"

But Megabat wasn't listening. He was too busy dancing up a storm.

He held his wings out, then crossed them over his body one at a time to make an *X* shape. "This is being the fanciest, goodliest dance!" he explained, as he moved his wings to his hips. He and Daniel had learned it in gym class. "It's being called the Macaroni!"

"With honeycombs!" the robot finished its joke, but Megabat shushed him.

"Watching!" He tucked his wings behind his head one after the other and swiveled his hips. Finally, Megabat clapped his wings together for the big finish. "Heeeeey, Macaroni!"

At first, the robot just blinked and Megabat assumed it was (understandably) impressed, but then it said, "That's funny." It laughed and laughed and laughed, rocking from side to side with all its buttons flashing.

"Stopping that!" Megabat ordered, but the robot blinked its big, bright eyes at Megabat and laughed some more.

"Oka-hay!" Megabat said sternly. "Mines had enough of yours for today! Going to the corner to thinking about yours's behavior." Megabat flew over to the robot controller the kids had left on the bed and started to steer it. The robot went in a straight line and bumped into the wall.

He backed it up and tried again. This time he managed to turn the robot, but it was headed straight for the stairs. He paused.

"I'm a great dancer too!" the robot said. "Do you want to watch me dance?"

Megabat couldn't take it one second longer—not just the braggy robot but everything unfair: how people said Daniel's face windows made him smart, but laughed at Megabat's twist-tie glasses; how Talia was strong, so she got to help with jobs, but he didn't; the way everyone got cheered and rewarded with a solid-gold trophy, a smelly sticker, a big birthday party or a shiny medal on a rope—everyone but him.

"Or I can tell you a joke. My jokes are hil-a-rious!" Boogie Bot trilled.

"Stop it, robot! Shushing up NOW!"

Megabat couldn't help himself. He pushed the forward button on the controller: full speed ahead.

THUNK! THUNK! THUNK! CRASH!

After that, the robot didn't have much to say at all.

BIG, BAD TROUBLE

The uh-oh feeling came right away.

Megabat tiptoed to the top of the stairs and peered down. Boogie Bot was lying on its back. Its legs were twitching in the air and—worst of all—one of its arms had snapped right off.

Megabat broke things a lot. He could think of three accidents in the last week alone. Just the day before, he'd ripped a library book called the *Big Book of Natural Disasters* when he'd been too eager to get to the page with the swirly tornado. (Daniel had to tape it back together, and the librarian was *not* going to be happy.) Then there was the Lego Starship Destroyer he'd flown off the shelf (Daniel fit the pieces back together, but it took hours), and the stuffed animal dinosaur he'd hugged too hard (Daniel's dad sewed the spike back on with a needle and thread).

Perhaps the robot could be fixed, like one of those things. Megabat flew down the stairs to examine it, but right away he knew it was useless. He wasn't good at fixing. Whenever he tried he got all

tangled in the tape, lost the smallest
Lego pieces or made knots in the string.

Fixing things took brains—and he
wasn't smart like Daniel.

He strained to lift the heavy robot arm
but couldn't. Megabat sighed. Sometimes,
fixing things also took muscles—and he
wasn't strong like Talia.

"Mine's also not the fanciest dancer," he admitted sadly to Boogie Bot. "Or the laughingest joker."

What *was* he good at—or good for? Megabat didn't know, and it gave him an empty feeling in his middle.

What's more, now that he had broken Daniel's best present, he was going to be in big, bad trouble.

"Mine is a rotten, good-at-nothing bat," he said to himself, and a big tear rolled down his face. "Daniel is deserving a better friend."

Boogie Bot twitched again. "Did someone say . . ." it began, but it couldn't finish the sentence. "Did someone s-s-s-say . . ."

"Undoubtedly!" Megabat cried. "Mine said mine's a bad, bad bat."

"I'm a . . . I'm a . . . I'm a great dancer . . ." stammered the robot.

"Yes, yes yours is!" Megabat agreed sadly.

"Ch-ch-ch-choose an option."

"What should mine do?" Megabat wailed.

"Do you want to do-do-do ballet?" the robot asked. "Or rumba-rumba-rumba-rumba . . ."

Megabat tiptoed closer and leaned down. "What's is yours trying to say, robot?"

"Rumba-rumba-rumba."

"Is yours trying to say *rumb-away*?"

Megabat's eyes went wide.

"Okay," the robot agreed.

Of course! Megabat could see that it was right! All the whispers Daniel and

Taila had been sharing suddenly made sense. He was being left out on purpose, because he wasn't good enough to be Daniel's friend! He *should* rumb-away. FOREVER.

"Ch-ch-choose an option. How about dis-co dis-co dis-co?" the robot stammered—which sounded an awful lot like *just go*, and so, wiping one last tear from his eye, Megabat did.

AN EXCELLENT
EXPLORATIONER

Megabat flew out the window and across
the yard, high over the heads of the
children, who were eating bowls of sugar
cereal at the picnic table. Unnoticed, he
swooped into the shed he shared with
Birdgirl and found a small suitcase on the
shelf where Daniel's parents kept the
tools.

After dumping out some odd metal bits, he filled it with his favorite things: his twist-tie face windows, his juice-box-straw lightsaber, a drawing Daniel had made of the two of them and half a peanut shell Birdgirl had given him that was shaped like a heart. Finally, he sat down on the floor with a stick to scratch a message in the dirt for his beloved.

With that, Megabat turned to go, but his gaze landed on a small package he'd tucked into the corner of the shed near the door. It was the birthday present that Birdgirl had helped him make for Daniel. He'd been planning to give it to his friend later that day, but now he was sure Daniel would be too angry to want it.

Megabat added it to his suitcase. It might come in handy. Then, fighting back tears, he tiptoed past the party guests, lugging the heavy case behind him. For a split second, Birdgirl, who was pecking at spilled cereal in the grass, glanced up at him. Megabat thought she might say "Coo-woooooo" (meaning, "Oh no, please don't go!"), but she only bobbed her head and went back to eating. Meanwhile, Daniel was far too busy smiling while his friends sang him a special happy-birthday song to notice the sad bat who turned and walked away.

Megabat journeyed alone for many minutes through the tall grass. The birdies were chirping and a warm breeze blew at his back.

"Perhaps," Megabat said to himself hopefully, after he'd stopped to sniff a small, white flower, "mine will make an excellent explorationer."

He and Daniel had seen an explorer's statue once at a park. The man was made of rock, but Daniel had explained that there had been a real person who

looked just like him. He'd set off bravely, traveled the world and seen many sights.

"Mine would make a most dustinguished statue," Megabat thought, already considering the pose his rock-self would strike. What's more, if he was a famous explorer, Daniel would certainly want to be his friend again!

The thought cheered Megabat as he made his way around tree roots and into a muddy patch. The first green shoots of tulips were peeking out. Exploring was fun and easy!

Only, before long, his tummy began to rumble.

"Greetings!" Megabat approached a little brown bird. "Mine is a traveler from a distant land. Where does yours keep the fruits?"

The bird cheeped. It pecked at the earth, pulled up a wriggling, grayish bug with two long rows of feet and dropped it in front of Megabat.

Megabat screwed up his snout. The birdie chirped and Megabat worried that

he'd hurt its feelings, so he quickly said,
"This is being yours's special footed-
food. Mine couldn't take it."

The bird shrugged, gobbled the
wriggler and cheeped goodbye.

Megabat journeyed on. He crossed
a large rock with many peaks, passed
beneath a tall wooden barrier and
ventured into a different land. There
were prickly, greenish bushes here and—
strangest of all—tiny people in pointed
hats who stood guard all around.

"Excusing mine," Megabat said as he
approached one. "Does yours knowing
where mine could find some fruits?"

The small, bearded man didn't answer.
Perhaps, Megabat thought, he hadn't

explained clearly. After all, the bird hadn't seemed to know what fruit was.

"Feetless fruits," Megabat added. "Suchly as buttermelons, bananas or grapes?"

The little man stared straight ahead, so Megabat tried the next pointy-hatted person. This one sat on a red mushroom, playing a long, shiny musical instrument. It reminded Megabat of the hummonica he so desperately wanted, and he had to blink back tears, remembering the birthday party he'd ruined, then left behind.

"Excusing mine, kind sir," Megabat began. But even though the person had large ears, he didn't seem to hear. Megabat went closer. He cupped his

wings around his snout and leaned in.
"EXCUSING MINE!" he shouted. That
was when he heard it.

Chichichichichi.

Not an answer from the small, hatted
person, but a chittering laugh.

Megabat didn't like being laughed at,
but he couldn't deny that it was nice to
see a familiar face. "Kwirl! What's is
yours doing in this strange land? Is yours
a friend of these small talkless peoples?"

Kwirl skittered down the fence and
picked a pebble out of the grass.
Megabat gasped when Kwirl threw it at
the little man's head, but Megabat
understood when it bounced off with a
sharp PING. The man didn't even flinch.

Chichichichi. Kwirl laughed, rolling
around in the grass.

"Of course! Mine knewed theys was
statues." Megabat tried to laugh like

Kwirl, but it came out funny. *"Chachacha.
Mine was joking yours. Undoubtedly.
It's being hil-a-rious."*

Kwirl twitched his tail. He turned
to scurry off, and Megabat felt his heart
lurch. He wanted to be an excellent
explorer, but the big wide world made
his feet hurt, his tummy grumble and
his whole self lonesome.

"Kwirl! Waiting!"

The squirrel stopped, turned,
chittered.

"Does yours gots any fruits?"

Kwirl shook his head.

"Peeze!"

The squirrel came slowly back down
the fence and toward Megabat. He

pointed at himself, then sniffed at the small suitcase that sat in the grass.

"Yours wants to do trade-sies for fruits?" Megabat asked.

Kwirl nodded.

"Fairly enough." Megabat opened the suitcase and showed Kwirl his best things. "Perhaps mine can interest yours in this fine nut pod."

Kwirl sniffed the heart-shaped peanut shell, but when he saw it was empty, he turned up his nose.

"Or this crafty drawing of Megabat and Daniel," Megabat offered, although he hated to part with it. Kwirl turned his back on the picture. He didn't like the twist-tie glasses either. And since there was no way Megabat could give away his juice-box-straw lightsaber (the first and best thing Daniel had ever given him), that left just one option.

"What abouting this present?" He held up the small package he'd wrapped in newspaper for Daniel. Megabat knew it for a fact: *everyone* likes presents.

Kwirl grabbed the package greedily and unwrapped it in a flurry of shredded paper. When he was done, he held up a floppy, gray fluff, tilting his head, clearly puzzled.

"It's being a nose beard," Megabat explained. "Alsowise known as a munkstash. A most dustinguished face decoration."

Megabat had decided to make the
mustache after Daniel said his teddy
bear was too babyish for an eight-year-
old. If teddy had a nose beard, like the
hairy one Daniel's father sometimes

sprouted on his upper lip—Megabat reasoned—it would be a most grown-up teddy indeed, and Daniel could keep cuddling it at night. Birdgirl had helped to pick out the very best dryer lint to build it from and to shape the ends into curls.

Kwirl tried it on. He sneezed three sneezes from the dusty lint, then went to peer at his reflection in a nearby puddle. He tilted his head this way and that, and must have been pleased with the effect because he nodded in Megabat's direction, as if inviting him to follow.

THE NEST

Megabat lugged his suitcase through the grass while Kwirl dashed ahead and circled back, always keeping Megabat in sight. They went under a fence and through a dense, weedy patch. Finally, Kwirl stopped in front of a bush with small, red berries.

They looked like fruit. Megabat rolled out his long tongue to test them but, at

the last second, sucked it back in. Long
ago, Talia had taught him never to eat
unfamiliar berries. They might be
poisonous. As rumbly as his tummy was,
he knew he shouldn't risk it.

"Gots any other fruits?" Megabat
asked, hopefully.

Kwirl shook his head.

Springtime was only beginning, and
Canada wasn't like the lush, green land
of Borneo, where Megabat had been
born. Here, there were seasons. Things
died and grew again.

Megabat was very hungry, and—worse
still—he looked up at the sky and saw
that darkness would be falling soon.

Just then, there was a strange fluttering,

flapping noise behind him. Megabat spun
on the spot, but there was nothing there.
Had it been a ghost? He wasn't sure, but
he didn't want to stick around to find out.
The air was cooling and he couldn't help
shivering—partly from cold and partly
from dread. As much as he hated to
admit it, Megabat was a little bit scared
of the dark.

"Does yours have a sleeping spot mine can share?" he asked Kwirl.

Kwirl waggled the nose beard, like he was considering it.

"Peeze?" Megabat made extra-big eyes.

Kwirl gave a little sigh, but he motioned to Megabat to follow. They crossed a mud puddle, passed beneath another barrier and finally emerged at the base of a big, strong tree.

Kwirl showed Megabat a spot between the roots where he could leave his suitcase. Then the squirrel climbed and Megabat flew. Up and up and up they went, above the garden fences, higher than the roofs of the houses and into the treetop. Finally, they came to a place where the trunk forked into two big branches, making a letter *Y*. Nestled in the *Y* was a ball-shaped nest built of mud, dried grass and leaves. From inside, Megabat could hear rustling. A soft-looking gray squirrel poked her head out a hole at the top. She spotted Kwirl and chittered loudly.

Kwirl chattered back, then began to strut along one branch. He waggled his new mustache a few times before spitting a seed out of his cheek. Then another and another, and even more still.

The gray squirrel hopped down to sniff the pile of seeds. She munched one, then packed the rest into her

cheeks and disappeared into the nest.
Megabat stood by awkwardly, waiting to
introduce himself.

A long minute later, she emerged again.

"Greetings," he said, with a little bow. "Mine is Megabat. Kwirl has broughtten mine for sharing yours's sleeping nest. Mine's most grateful for your hoppitality."

The gray squirrel chittered something at Kwirl, who shrugged, pointed at his new mustache, motioned into the distance and chattered something back. Megabat guessed they were discussing the handsomeness of the nose beard. He didn't mean to interrupt, but his tummy was grumbling loudly.

"Excusing mine," he said. "But Megabat is most snacky. Before sleeping time, does yours have any foods mine can eat?"

The gray squirrel dug around in her cheek with her tongue and spat out a slimy seed at Megabat's feet.

He jumped back in disgust, then he remembered his manners. "Thanking yours kindly, but mine is only eating fruits."

The squirrel tilted her head in a question, so he explained. "Foods of a sweetish kind, having delicious juicy ooze."

She cheeped something at Kwirl before scurrying down the tree.

Should Megabat follow? It seemed like the right thing to do. Round and round the tree she ran and Megabat flew down behind her. When they reached

the bottom branches, she pointed toward a small hole in the tree. Megabat approached it, sniffing.

There was a wet patch on the bark that had a familiar smell—like the pancakes Daniel's mother made for special breakfasts. But why would a tree smell like pancakes?

Of course! "Maple sweerup sap!" Megabat unrolled his long tongue and ate hungrily until his tummy grew rolly-polly. When he finished, he leaned back on the tree branch and let out a huge burp. "Thanking yours," Megabat said to the gray squirrel. But instead of saying "yours is welcome," in squirrel language, she made a motion that Megabat had seen Kwirl do—pointing at herself with one paw.

"Yours wants a trade?" Megabat asked.

The squirrel led Megabat back up the tree. When they reached the *Y*-shaped branches, she pointed at the nest. Did she want him to help clean it, the way they cleaned Daniel's room on Sundays, sorting Lego into bins and gathering socks off the floor?

The gray squirrel chittered, and Kwirl came out of the nest—but he wasn't alone! There was a much smaller squirrel perched on his head, and two more tiny ones tugging his tail.

"Kwirl!" Megabat said. "Yours is being a daddy?"

The gray squirrel pointed at the nest again, then at Megabat. "Yours wants mine to going inside?"

She nodded. Next, she dashed down the tree. She returned a minute later, wearing a fancy hat made from an upside-down flower.

Megabat wasn't a fan of clean-up time. Still, a trade was a trade. He climbed into the nest, ready to help tidy. But before he could start looking for dirty socks a baby squirrel fell on his head, then another and another.

"Stopping!" Megabat called. He flapped out of the nest hole. "Coming back!" he yelled—as he realized what was happening. But the adult squirrels just looked over their shoulders and waved as they headed off for a lovely evening out.

"But waiting!" Megabat wailed. "Mine's never kwirl-sitted before!"

KWIRL-SITTING

The first Thursday of every month
Daniel's parents bought fancy ingredients,
put on nicer-than-normal clothes, and
went to their cookbook book club.

On these nights, a tall girl named
Devan came to babysit. At first, Daniel
had been afraid of her, but he and
Megabat soon saw that she was excellent.
She let Daniel eat snacks wherever he

wanted—even on the good sofa. She had lots of ideas for games, and she let Daniel stay up way past bedtime.

Perhaps, Megabat thought, as he blinked at the baby squirrels and they blinked back, he knew more than he'd at first thought. In fact, he might make the world's best kwirl-sitter!

"Greetings, mini-kwirls," he said. Then, to show how friendly he was, Megabat gave the babies his biggest, battiest smile, showing all his fangs.

Right away, they started crying.

"Stop! Stop! Stopping it!" Megabat ordered. "Stopping crying!" He looked around desperately for something to distract them. "Aha." His eyes landed on

the pile of spitty seeds the mother
squirrel had left in the nest.

He picked one up with his wingtip.
"Yugh," he muttered. "Oka-hay. Here
are being the rules." Megabat had to
shout to be heard over the crying. "Mine
will throwing the seeds, and yours will
catching thems with yours's faces."

It was like the Corn-Pops Toss game at Daniel's birthday party only, this time, Megabat would get to play too.

"The mini-kwirl who catches the mostest will winning the grandest prize."

The babies stopped crying. They were looking at him eagerly. Two of them already had their mouths open, so Megabat began throwing seeds. Left and right, they dodged, dove and climbed over each other to catch them. The game went on for some time and, as Megabat neared the bottom of the pile, it was clear to him that the miniest of the mini-squirrels was definitely the winner.

"Splendiferous catching!" Megabat congratulated her. But instead of basking in the compliment, she held out her paw like she was waiting for something.

Chichichi. She frowned. *Chichichi.*

"Huh? Oh! The grandest prize." Megabat had nearly forgotten about that part. "Waiting here." He popped out of the nest. Up so high in the treetops there wasn't much to be found. Only budding leaves and more budding leaves and, "Aha!" Megabat spotted something that might do.

He flew back into the nest.

"What's being brown and sticky?" The baby squirrels waited eagerly. "Ta-daaah! A stick!" He produced it from behind his back. "Getting it? It's being a joke."

They didn't seem to get it.

The smallest squirrel sniffed the twig, then she gnawed it. She pushed it aside. Her brother picked it up and used it to poke her in the tummy, then into his brother's eye. Soon, everyone was crying again.

"Stoppit. Stopping it," Megabat said, but none of the squirrels were listening. "SHUSHING!" he yelled, finally. He grabbed the stick back. The baby squirrels whimpered and whined.

Luckily, Megabat knew one last babysitting trick—something no kid could resist. "Let's be playing another game. This one's being called Waaaay-Past-Bedtime Tag."

The babysitter named Devan played it

with Daniel. After he'd brushed his teeth and put on pajamas, they ran up and down the stairs and jumped across the furniture until, finally, Daniel got so tired that he'd ask to go to bed. When Daniel's parents came home, they always said what a good job Devan had done. They even gave her money and asked her to come again. If Megabat wore the mini-squirrels out, the parents would chitter in appreciation. Surely, he'd be the best kwirl-sitter they'd ever had!

"Tag! Yours is it!" Megabat tapped the smallest squirrel.

The babies took off, dashing around the tree and leaping from branch to branch to branch.

Chichichichichi.

They tagged each other, laughed, then ran out of sight again.

The game was a huge success. Way-Past-Bedtime Tag kept the baby kwirls so busy, in fact, that Megabat had time to sit on a tree branch and clean his talons, which were dirty from such a long day of adventuring.

Chichichi. Zoom!

Chichichi. Leap!

Megabat was licking out a particularly sticky bit of ugh from between his talons when—*Chichichichi* Weeeeeeee!—a squirrel-shaped blur whizzed past him and ran straight off the end of the branch.

In an instant, Megabat could see that the baby was in trouble. He flung out his super-long tongue.

Snap.

He wrapped it around the tumbling mini-squirrel in the nick of time, but before he could begin to reel his tongue in to bring the baby to safety, he felt a grabby paw on his shoulder.

He turned to see an angry-looking Kwirl. With the baby still wrapped in his tongue, Megabat could only wave a meek "Welcome home" with one wingtip.

And instead of saying "Thanking yours for playing fun games with ours's babies" in their chittery squirrel

language, mother squirrel crossed her
arms, and daddy Kwirl frowned deeply
beneath his mustache.

CLOCK PIE

The squirrel parents did *not* pay Megabat money. They did *not* ask him to come back again. Instead, they gathered their babies and took them into the nest, then Kwirl pointed to a cold, lonely crevice in the tree where Megabat could sleep.

Megabat did *not* sleep.

A cold wind whistled around the tree, and the leaves made strange, shifting

shadows all night long. Twice, he thought
he heard an eerie flapping sound.

"Who-who-who-whose is there?" he
said in a shaky voice . . . but the only
answer was a faint oooo-woooo and a
rustling of leaves. Megabat backed
farther into his tree crevice and opened
his eyes even wider to keep watch.

Finally, just as the sun was coming up,
a very weary Megabat couldn't stay
awake a second longer. He drifted off
into a fitful sleep until—

"What are we going to do if Megabat
doesn't come back in time?"

At the sound of his name, Megabat's
eyelids popped open. His heart leapt. It
was Talia's voice! But what was his friend

doing in this strange land, so far from home?

Megabat tiptoed to the edge of a branch and peered over. Daniel was there too! So were Birdgirl and Priscilla the cat!

And—Megabat blinked in surprise—down below were a familiar shed and house. He was certain he'd journeyed many miles but, in fact, he'd only circled the neighboring yards and ended up in a big tree whose branches overhung Daniel's fence.

Daniel sighed heavily. "The whole thing's going to be a disaster," he told Talia.

A disaster? Megabat leaned forward to hear better. What kind of disaster?

He'd learned about many kinds before
he'd ripped Daniel's library book.
Earthquakes made the ground rumble.
Tsunamis sent a huge wave out of the
sea. In a volcano, fire shot out of a big
mountain. But there were no seas or
mountains near Daniel's house.

"Should we put these up just in case?"
Talia was holding two rolls of rope-ish
stuff. One orange and one yellow. The
colors reminded Megabat of the safety
vest the school crossing guard wore.

"Yeah," Daniel said. "I guess so." He
took one end of the yellow rope and
started to walk across the lawn with it,
looping it over the fence every so often
as he went.

"What else should we do to get ready?" Talia asked. "I've got the special hats."

Megabat scritched his head. Special hats? Did they mean hard hats like the ones workers wore on construction sites? What could this disaster be?

"That's good. After we put them on, we should get the food and drinks sorted out," Daniel added.

Two yards over a lawn mower started up. Megabat frowned and leaned forward even more, but now he could only catch a few words over the roaring noise.

"Stuff to do . . ."

"Start at ten-thirty—like . . ."

"Twister."

Twister! That was another word for tornado. A very serious disaster indeed! Gathering food and drinks to wait out the storm was a good idea. But why were Daniel and Talia roping off the yard and putting on special hats? What they needed to do was get inside to safety by ten-thirty! The best place to be was a basement.

If they weren't going to get inside themselves, Megabat would have to rescue them. And—best of all, he realized—if he saved the day, Daniel would surely forgive him for breaking the robot and ruining the birthday party!

Only, how was he supposed to know when ten-thirty was?

There was a clock on the kitchen wall inside Daniel's house. But Megabat was no good at telling time. What if he got it wrong again?

He had to try.

As Daniel and Talia continued to put up their silly safety strings, Megabat

swooped high above them across the yard
and landed on the kitchen windowsill.

There was the clock, hanging on the
wall beside the oven. Megabat studied it
carefully. It was big and round like a
pizza, with twelve numbers on it.

Megabat didn't like pizza. Perhaps if he imagined pie instead. Yes, a fruit pie! Only, what flavor? Lemon? Too sour. Apple? So nice, but apples grew in the fall. Aha! Daniel's father had just brought sweet, ripe cherries home from the market. Cherries were a springtime fruit. Megabat licked his lips and considered the clock hungrily.

"Twelvish pieces of oozy cherry pie."

The baby hand of the clock was near the ten. That part was easy. It meant ten o'clock. But now it was time to do the minutes, and those were what got him in trouble last time.

Megabat frowned, then squinted. What was this? Between each number on the clock there were little lines. He counted them. Five for each number.

"Perhapsing each slice takeses five minutes to eat," he muttered to himself. He imagined the reddish sweetness on his tongue. "One slice makeses five minutes. One mores makeses ten minutes of delicious snacking. Mmmmmm . . . Three tasty triangles giveses fifteen minutes of munching."

He kept going, counting by fives all the way to where the biggish hand was resting on the number five. "Aha! Twenty-five minutes of squishy, scrumptious pie." He licked his lips, thinking of all that juicy goodness. Would there be strawberry ice cream with the pie too? Then Megabat gasped.

One more piece would make ten-thirty. Tornado time! He had to warn Talia and Daniel.

Quick as a flash, he flew into the backyard.

"Daniel! Talia! Birdgirl! Priscilla!" he cried. "Getting inside now! Be being careful of the twister! It's is being . . ." but before he could get out the words *ten-thirty*, his friends all spotted him and shouted:

"SURPRISE!"

THE SURPRISE PARTY

Megabat's mouth dropped open so wide that his tongue rolled out.

Everyone was there! They were all wearing pointy hats. Daniel, Talia, Birdgirl . . . even Priscilla the cat. The yellow and orange streamers were looped all around the fence. And there were balloons now! Green ones! Plus a big paper banner that read *Happy Batday!*

"Just because we don't know when your birthday is doesn't mean you can't have a *batday*," Daniel explained, when he saw Megabat reading the sign.

"We gathered all your favorite things," Talia went on excitedly. She pointed to a feast of fruit on the picnic table: buttermelon, oranges, strawberries and mangoes. "Birdgirl even made hats from old wrapping paper and string. And we're going to play Twister. We know how much you like that game." She motioned to a box lying on the ground.

Twister! It was the game with colorful dots. The one that had a spinner Megabat loved to sit in the middle of and ride around on.

That's what Daniel and Talia had meant all along. There was no tornado. No disaster at all!

"We've been planning it for days. It's why we've been whispering so much. And why we wanted to save all the green balloons," Daniel added. "Just for you!"

Megabat sank down on the grass as he tried to take it all in. "Yours maked mine a whole party?" He looked around at the beautiful decorations and shook his head. "And mine almost missed it by rumbing-away. Forever!"

"We were pretty sure you'd come back in time," Talia said. "Plus, Birdgirl was keeping an eye on you, so we knew you were safe."

Those strange flapping sounds and
the oooo-woooo all made sense now.
Megabat suddenly felt very silly, and
very small. A tear escaped his eye and
trickled down his cheek.

"What's wrong, Megabat?" Daniel asked. "Don't you like your surprise party?"

"Mine loves mine's sumprise party!" Megabat wailed.

"Why are you so sad, then?" Talia asked.

"Because mine didn't saving the day."

"What do you mean, Megabat?"

He explained about hearing them say twister, and how he'd gone to read the clock to warn them of the disaster in time. "But mine's no hero," Megabat cried. "Alsowise, mine's not the best joker or dancer or adventurer or kwirl-sitter. Mine can't even rumb-away right!"

144

"So what?" Daniel said. "Why do those things even matter?"

"Because . . ." Megabat sniffed. "Daniel is being the smartest, and Talia is being the strongest, and Birdgirl is being the craftiest." He rubbed his eyes and looked at the cat, who was flouncing around, rubbing her fluffy face on the legs of the picnic table. "And cat is being the fanciest. But mine is being the nothingest!" Megabat dissolved into blubbering tears.

"But Megabat . . ." Daniel said gently. "You've got plenty of gifts."

Megabat blinked. He didn't see any.

"I don't mean presents. I mean stuff you're good at. People call those gifts too. And you've got loads."

"Mine does?"

"I mean. Yeah!" Talia said. "For example, you're a really good hider."

"Grown-ups hardly ever spot you. Plus," Daniel added a second later, "you're a great burper! I've never met someone so small who could burp so loud."

This was true. But compared to being the strongest or the smartest, being the hidingest burper didn't seem very wonderful. Megabat started to cry again.

"And you're great at figuring stuff out," Daniel went on. "You just taught yourself how to tell time! It took me ages to learn that. I shouldn't have gotten mad at you before at the sugar bush—telling time is hard."

"Plus, you can read and write . . . and talk!" Talia pointed out. "How many bats can do that?"

"Yours is trying to make mine feeling better, but it's being none use," Megabat wailed. "Mine is good for nothing. A bad, bad bat. Mine isn't goodly enough for being yours's friend."

"Megabat!" Daniel gasped. "Is *that* why you ran away?"

"Undoubtedly," Megabat said with a little sniff.

"You're not a bad bat!" Daniel said. "Sure, breaking the robot was a bad thing to do—but everyone makes mistakes."

"Definitely," Talia agreed. "I mean,

I'm strong, but I don't land all my flips in gymnastics. Sometimes I fall."

"And even though I get better grades now that I can see the board with my glasses, I still get words wrong on my spelling test sometimes," Daniel added. "Like *knife*. Did you know it starts with a *K*? That doesn't even make sense."

"Nife . . . Nnnnnnnife." Megabat sounded it out. "There's none kuh sound." He was outraged on Daniel's behalf. "That's being SO none fair!"

"That's what I told Mrs. Gallagher," Daniel said. "But she wouldn't give me the point. Anyway . . ." Daniel continued, "I think I kind of owe you an apology. About my birthday party."

Megabat tilted his head in confusion.

"It's still wrong that you broke my robot. But I think I get why you did it. I wasn't making you feel included. Every guest at a party should get to have fun and feel special, even secret guests. Do you forgive me?"

Megabat flapped up from the grass, launched himself at Daniel's face and gave his nose a big hug.

"Of coursing mine forgives yours! Does yours forgives mine?"

Daniel laughed. He plucked Megabat off his face and balanced him in one palm. "Yes. Always. You know you're the best bat friend a kid could ever ask for, right?"

Megabat's large ears perked up. "The
best bat friend?"

"Yeah," Daniel said.

Megabat wiped the tears from his
eyes. Then he clasped his wingtips
behind his back and looked up at Daniel

hopefully. "Is there being a splendiferous prize for thats?" He was already imagining a large, glistening trophy with a tiny golden bat perched on top.

"Well, no," Daniel said. "But, if there was, you'd definitely win it."

The little bat tried hard not to look too disappointed.

"We do have a present for you though," Talia said brightly.

Daniel ran inside to get it. A moment later, he was back with a small, colorfully wrapped package.

"Open it!" he urged.

Daniel, Talia, Birdgirl and the cat all gathered around to watch as Megabat tore at the paper with his fangs.

"Yours has *gots* to be kidding mine! A HUMMONICA!" Megabat cried, when the present was revealed in all its shiny silver glory.

After that, the party *really* got started. Megabat played song after song after song, inventing them as he went. Each one was louder and hummier than the last. The kwirl family—awoken from their sleep—came down from the tree to listen. Next, there was a jelly roll with candles in it. And before Megabat blew them out, everyone sang a happy-batday song, just for him.

"Talia and I were thinking you and Birdgirl and the squirrels could do gloop gliding now," Daniel suggested, once

their tummies were full of jelly roll and fruit.

"Perhapsing not," Megabat said. He loved to slide in slippery stuff, and he didn't mind getting sticky, but it wasn't as much fun for Daniel and Talia, who only got to watch. And the cat hated to get dirty.

Like Daniel said, *every* guest should feel included and have fun at a party.

"Should we play Twister, then?" Daniel asked, but Megabat shook his head. Even Twister had winners and losers, and he'd had enough of that for the next little while.

"Mine has a muchly better idea." He picked up the harmonica and started to play it again, but Daniel didn't seem to recognize the tune. "Listening, Daniel!" he said, before taking another breath. "Listening to the Macaroni!"

Daniel laughed and started the moves.

Then everyone—including the baby squirrels and the little brown bird— gathered on the lawn to learn the fanciest, goodliest dance. And even though it was Megabat's first-ever bat day, he already had a feeling it would be his best.

A Little Bit about Bats

Megabat is based on a real kind of fruit bat (or megabat) called the lesser short-nosed fruit bat. These bats are tiny, weighing between 21 and 32 grams—which is about as heavy as an AA battery, or a mouse—and live in South and Southeast Asia and Indonesia (Borneo), usually in rainforests, near gardens, near vegetation or on beaches.

Of course, even though Megabat is based on a real kind of bat, he's also made up. I don't need to tell you that actual bats can't talk . . . not even in the funny way that Megabat talks! But it might be worth mentioning that bats don't make good pets, either.

Bats are amazing creatures and an important part of our ecosystem. North American bats eat insects, and they're rarely dangerous to humans. So if you see a bat in the wild it's okay to observe it from a distance, but don't try to touch it or trap it!

Acknowledgments

When I started this series, I never dreamed my little bat would travel so far or have such big fans. I owe a great big thanking yours to all the readers— young and young-at-heart. There's nothing quite like knowing Megabat has been a part of your classroom, your bedtime stories and your lazy Saturday afternoons.

As always, big batty high-fives to all the people who make these books possible: including Sam Swenson, Sam Devotta, John Martz and the rest of the team at Tundra Books; Amy Tompkins (agent extraordinaire); and Kass Reich (whose drawings just keep getting cuter and cuter and unbelievably cuter still.)

And, of course, kudos to my family, who might roll their eyes every now and then, but continue to gamely answer questions like: "If you were a bat, what would you most want for a birthday present?" Brent, Grace and Elliot: you guys get me, and that's not always easy to do.

ANNA HUMPHREY has worked in marketing for a poetry organization, in communications for the Girl Guides of Canada, as an editor for a webzine, as an intern at a decorating magazine and for the government. None of those was quite right, so she started her own freelance writing and editing business on top of writing for kids and teens. She lives in a big, old brick house in Kitchener, Ontario, with her husband and two kids and no bats. Yet.

KASS REICH was born in Montreal, Quebec. She works as an artist and educator and has spent the majority of the last decade traveling and living abroad. She now finds herself back in Canada, but this time in Toronto. Kass loves illustrating books for all ages, like *Carson Crosses Canada*, *Sergeant Billy* and *Hamsters Holding Hands*.